A HORRiBLE NIGHT SEASON 1

HEMILKUMAR P PATEL

ISBN 978-93-5610-467-9
© HEMILKUMAR P PATEL 2022
Published in India 2022 by Pencil

Contributors:
Co-Author: HEMILKUMAR P PATEL

A brand of
One Point Six Technologies Pvt. Ltd.
123, Building J2, Shram Seva Premises,
Wadala Truck Terminal, Wadala (E)
Mumbai 400037, Maharashtra, INDIA
E connect@thepencilapp.com
W www.thepencilapp.com

DISCLAIMER: *The opinions expressed in this book are those of the authors and do not purport to reflect the views of the Publisher.*

Author biography

What time is it and what is our society? If no one speaks, then when the time comes, such a person also comes to help. Funny thing is don't know what will happen to people tomorrow then some people become naive then some people become clever. Clever will look good in the job and business, then naive people cheating.

like

It was something like that day,

Quitting can be a compulsion,

But not because of any flaws in the relationship,

Maybe her ears were thirsty or someone,

Quenching the thirst of the ears.

Quenching the thirst of the ears has ruined a lot of relationships, let's try to improve.

CONTENTS

A HORRIBLE NIGHT SEASON 1

Part 1 : The subject of research

Part 2 : Satish's talk

Part 3 : Advent of Satish and beginning of Rahi

Part 4 : Rahi's love story

Part 5 : Start Game, wait and watch.

Part 6 : Rahi and Ashish meet

Part 7 : The fact of Rahi

Part 8 : Ravi's talk

Part 9 : The secret of Ravi

Part 10 : Rahi's mysterious story.

ONE CHARACTER SAY : Your thoughts will be waiting and these are the thoughts I am going to give to the world. If you don't help I'll do it alone, But in this college and also in other colleges, when someone wakes up and responds verbally to correct the boy, these people will know about a girl and her house. Only then will I be very happy inside, I didn't think much about my house before doing this, I just thought Nirbhaya case,Nine month old girl, Doctor's rap, Then the rap-taking advantage of such a national politics chair, In this, everyone's house cried for the rest of their lives. And with my help, if any house survives, I will do and will continue to do. This is the culture of India I will try to improve till my last breath because the soul of all the raped girls is with me, I don't care if you don't stay. If I start the game, I will finish for them, I will show the world what is wrong and what is true, just change the idea, a lot will change.

Part 1 The subject of research

What time is it and what is our society? If no one speaks, then when the time comes, such a person also comes to help. Funny thing is don't know what will happen to people tomorrow then some people become naive then some people become clever. Clever will look good in the job and business, then naive people cheating.

like

It was something like that day,

Quitting can be a compulsion,

But not because of any flaws in the relationship,

Maybe her ears were thirsty or someone,

Quenching the thirst of the ears.

Quenching the thirst of the ears has ruined a lot of relationships, let's try to improve.

23 MARCH 2024

A boy is sleeping in the house and suddenly he has a bad dream, If a Humans in the cemetery is burning, if someone looks strange, if someone sees him walking away in a dream, he immediately screams and comes to his senses,Whose name is Satish,Satish is 28 years old,

His housemaid comes screaming.And this Satish lives in Ahmedabad in Gujarat.Satish goes to the hospital after drinking tea after asking tea from the maid without saying anything.Standing outside the ICU in the hospital, he sees someone through an open glass and tears well up in his eyes.Tears well up in his eyes and he sees some boys coming, so he takes the chocolate out of his bag and gives it to them.

"Eat chocolate, boys and girls." Satish said.

"Thank you." Said one girl.

"Yes, take this speedily. Everyone will get it. " Satish said.

"Uncle, why do you share chocolates?" Said one girl.

"What's your name?" Satish said.

"My name is Rashmita." Rashmita said.

"Rashmita, today is my sister Rahi's birthday." Satish said.

"Where is she? I want to wish her." Rashmita said.

As soon as he said this, Satish's face became sad. It's as if something big is missing or someone is missing.

"She is not in this world." Satish said in a sad voice.

"Sorry. But what happened to Aunty, can you tell me? " Rashmita said.

"Back to the memories! Come on, let me tell you the whole story." Satish said.

(Past 1)

25 February 2020

[Gujarat, this is the city where people come to earn money, There is a journalist who just wants to come to Gujarat and do something new, It is a matter of time.

Tonight,

On such a night, there was a house in a deserted place in Umargam, which connects Maharashtra a little far from Gujarat.There is something to know. A long time ago, someone died or was killed in this house. If a man does not have any news, the journalist thinks that if I bring this news out, it will become my name.But he has no idea about the place.Then it happens that he stays inside the house at night.He looks around a lot as he walks into the house.A little bit goes inside and immediately the door closes, If this happens then it is scary,Yet with courage he slowly goes inside. He hears the sound of glass breaking. Sweat dripped from his forehead. He has a camera in his hand and goes home. Something appears in the camera but no one is in front. Then he sees something that suddenly screams.Then it disappears in such a way that it is eaten by the sky or the ground?How?What night was the ghost?Maybe then the curse is on.Don't know anything.

At the same time, happiness has been looted from Jatin's house.]

Beginning characters

Jayesh: The head of the house,

Jatin: Jayesh's son.

Satish: Jayesh's son has gone to Kolkata to study,

Reshma: Jatin's wife,

Nikhil: Police officer,

Rahi: Jatin's daughter.

(Everyone is sitting quietly at Jatin's house.The family lives in a large palace-like building in Vapi City.His wife is crying,Jatin's father hugs him and sits quietly,Nikhil is sitting in front of Jatin.And his daughter Rahi has been missing for a few days.)

"Nothing will happen now,How long will I look for my daughter,But there is no alternative but to find it. "Jatin said looking in front of his father and police officer Nikhil.

"Hey, after knowing everything, you will get some information about Rahi,We just asked her friend and thought she would get it or that is not found,You have to be patient. "Nikhil explains that Jatin calms down.

"Everything will be fine, son.What happens to our daughter,This can be a little time consuming,The magic is of time, Will be found.What happens to our Rahi,Rahi's nature was to win everyone's heart."Jayesh explains to his daughter-in-law.

At the same time, Jatin gets a call.But Jatin can't speak and then tries to speak.

"Satish's phone has come."Jatin said looking in front of his wife.

"Don't tell her anything."Reshma speaks in a roaring voice.

"Hello," Jatin picked up the phone and spoke.Jatin also had to take care of the grief.

Satish has gone to study in Kolkata.

"Hello, Dad, how are you?"Satish said.

"Just fine son, when will your study be over?"Jatin said.

"Dad called for that.My three month experience will be completed in eight days and then I will come."Satish said happily.

"Yes, come soon,We are all waiting."Jatin said a little loosely.

"Dad,Be prepared for the reception.I will go to college ready now.Just eight days, remember."Satish said happily.

"Yes, son. Let's take care of it."Jatin and Satish both put down the phone after talking so much.

"Comes after eight days."Jatin's words made the whole family tense.

"How do we explain that?"Reshma speaks in a sad voice.

"Hard situation, If he doesn't see Rahi coming now, he will be in trouble.That's right, he will say, why didn't you say first,Why hide it? "Jayesh looked at Jatin andsaid.

"Nothing to say right now,Will know later,Let's just say-He will not stay there."Jatin stands up and speaks.

"It's okay to come after knowing everything."Jayesh said. "Nikhil sir, let's go back to Shimla,And overall, maybe something will be found. "Jatin said looking at Nikhil.

"There's no point in going,The hotel has been cleaned by bringing everything here from there.It has been three months since Rahi disappeared from Shimla.All that is left is the work of the brain."Nikhil said.

"My only daughter,People who went with her today say she disappeared.They say an animal took my daughter.

Where is my daughter today?I had to think a lot for her life.When she came into the world, we all followed him,If she got angry for something after making fun of her, she would bring her up immediately.Now that she was of marriageable age, I kept thinking about everything.I kept thinking about how to prepare.But the question is, where did my daughter stay in the crowd of this world?"Jatin said, suddenly bursts into tears.Jayesh goes to him to calm him down.

"By accepting certain things, Have to move on. I don't know if it disappeared, But what was supposed to happen happened,What an advantage in thinking more now? Jayesh said.

"If Satish comes, he has to be explained, otherwise it will be difficult to save him."Reshma said.

"Leave it all,Don't think too slowly, Jatin,We are trying our best.Now nothing seems to come from Shimla. You have to see a few relationships in college.Let me go now.I'll call if I find anything."Nikhil said.

"Yes, of course."Jatin said.

Thinking that something bad has happened, Jatin drinks alcohol at night and thinks that everything has happened.

It's not hard to get, So losing is not the same thing

It doesn't take long to build a house, it doesn't take long to build a house,

The hospital comes to take all the medicine for every pain,

But losing oneself does not cause great pain.

Let's decorate the house,

So I don't know that nature takes revenge for any mistake, Yes, yes.

....

Part 2 : Satish's talk

(Kolkata)

Satish's face is smiling as he puts down the phone.

"Ravi,Come fast."Satish calls Ravi,Who is Satish's servant.

This Ravi's appearance is something like this, he is nine years older than Satish and has a big beard, There are a few cuts on the mouth,One eye is brown, As if something had attacked, But by nature he is good and simple. Then he comes with Satish from the kitchen.

"Yes sir."Ravi looks in front of Satish and said.

"How many times have I told you not to tell me sir?Forget that you are older than me!"Satish said.

"Yes, Satish, was there any work?"Ravisaid.

"Hey sit, I have something to say to you here with me."Satish catches Ravi and speaks while sitting.

"Yes, yes, sit down,You are very happy today brother,What is the reason for this happiness? "Ravi said.

"Hey,I have to finish my studies in eight days.So now I am going home after many year."Satish said happily.

"The best thing to say is,It is best to study in such a way that no time is wasted."Ravi said.

"Hey, a lot of people like me are studying.Living with you, I have learned a lot.You helped me with what I didn't like.We should know whether you were educated or not but you are very intelligent and proud of you my dear friend."Satish said happily.

"It simply came to our notice then.Let's start preparing slowly now,You don't have much time."Ravi said.

"Whether it's time or not, I'm thinking of something special for you."Satish said.

"What's that?"Ravi said.

"I have a party tonight with my friend, Our people are not the whole college.You have to come with me too.DJ has a party with ten or twelve people at the hotel.Enjoy tonight maybe your name? "Satish said.

Night, Satish and Ravi leave to go to the hotel. Once there, songs are played. Satish organizes the whole party, Yet he finally arrives, And a small stage is created he goes on stage and speaks.

"I am Satish,You know you don't play, you don't clap, you don't joke.Let's all get together in the last time to organize this party.After a few days, everyone has one thing in mind, our future is to be created.We will all be under the pressure of this, that is, under the pressure of creating the future.Sometimes if we meet on the road, we will talk, but nothing.I don't want to be upset by all this.I have planned the party for Ravi only. "Satish said.

(Ravi looks at him in amazement)

"Yes, Ravi is just for you.I told you today is a special day for you.It seemed to me that Ravi was a part of my house.We didn't know each other.What happened seven or eight months ago?

(Past 2)

I left home that day to go to college.So my shoes are torn,Went to sew.At that time Ravi was sitting a little away from the college.And I went to him.

'Brother, this shoe is torn. Please fix it.'said.

'Yes, why not!If You Don't Mind,I will take it. Everyone has the right to life as per Article 19 but some peoplecannot see us sitting here.'Ravi said.

(Present, past 1)

Speaking of which, I feel that Ravi is educated.Then I asked everything,It had noneAnd my servant wanted a higher salary.This Ravi was all about housework,So I called her at my house.He would then help with both the housework and my study.If I didn't know, I would learn with him,He knows everything.In my house it felt like someone in this house lived for me.Even if it hurts, he would take careand Ravi helped me all this. I have always considered you as my elder brother. Ravi Brother, I dare to speak today in front of you,Today you listen to me.No one belongs to anyone,I have seen so much in this world,But you continued to help me without committing a single sin.You did not even love money to serve me.You must have thought I was leaving.So you have to do such a job somewhere else.Hey, I'm going home. If I consider you big brother, can't I take you home? "Satishsaid.

"But how can I be at your house?"Ravi said.

"This is my time, You can do a lot of work for me,So it is my duty to give you something,So I call you my big brother and take him along I don't want anything else. Just let me do that, brother."Satish said.

"Yes, brother, that's all there is to it."Ravi said.

("My long running game will now be over by breaking into Satish's house, It will be fun. " Ravi smiled and said in his mind.)

"Let's party now." Satish said.

After Satish, all the friends are having fun together. Ravi also has fun. Also drinks a lot of alcohol, Live as if it were the last day. This is how other days go,Everything is packed. Ravi and Satish then look around the house, lock the house and leave for Gujarat to go to his house.

....

Part 3 : Advent of Satish and beginning of Rahi

4 March 2020

Satish comes to his house with Ravi. The doorbell rang. And Satish's mom opens the door.

"Hey Satish."Reshma said happily and Satish will be too.

"Mommy. I missed them so much."Satish comes home talking and Ravi also comes.

"We were remembering.And who is this brother?"Reshma said looking at Ravi.

"Hey, what I said, Ravi does, joins me, this man.He helped me a lot. "Satish said.

"Come on, son, this house is our understanding."Reshma said.

"Yes, the house is very nice."Ravi said.

"How are you, Grandpa and Dad?Everything runs smoothly!"Satish said.

"Yes, yes, everything is fine."When Jatin said in a low voice, Satish became suspicious.

"Why did low voice speak?Is there a problem?Where is Rahi?"Satish saying this, everyone calms down.

"What happened?"Satish said.

"Hey, there's nothing new. If you talk fresh, then it will happen."Jayesh said.

"Where are you hiding something?"Satishsaid sharply.

That's why he sees a few tears in his mother's eyes.

"Dad, tell me the truth, what happened?"Satishsaid,"Rahi rahi, where are you?" Screaming all over the house, no answer.

"Dad, what happened? Do you want to hide it?"Satishsaid.

Ravi also depresses a bit.

"Not Rahi."Jayesh said.

"Where is it?" Satish said.The question has not crossed Satish's mind.

"We don't know." Jatinsaid in a low voice.

"Why don't you know what happened?" Satish said in a slightly sharp voice.

"We don't even know." Jatin said.

"Don't bother me by saying I don't know, please tell me what happened?" Satish said.

"Our Rahi,It was the year of college and suddenly time started playing on his head.Our Rahi was very happyBut all of a sudden, things went awry." Jatin said.

"Tell us what's wrong."When Ravi said like this, everyone started looking in front of him."Hey, if Satish calls me Brother, then I will consider Rahi as Sister."

"Rahi can't wait, Satish. Listen now."Jatin said.

(Then Jatin talks about a year ago.)

(Past 2)

20 March 2019

"Years ago, Rahi was fond of the environment,So she took admission in Environment of Valsad Gujarat.I wanted to give her favorite college and education,Rahi was very happy at that time.Rahi's first day was in college and she went to college.Now if there is a college, there is going to be sisterhood. So she became two special sisterhood, one was Rita and the other was Bansi. They lived together in college.Rita's brother Mahesh took good care of these threeAnd they were all having breakfast in the canteen one day. It is a matter of time."Jatin said of the past.

(Mahesh and three sisterhood are sitting in the canteen, Because of Mahesh's good nature And since there is no sin in the heart, all are together.)

"Rahi, what are you doing, my sisterhood and sister?" Mahesh said.

"Mahesh, don't look back,There are four boys in the back who are constantly looking in front of me.When I come to college from outside, those people are standing on the bike by the door, sitting on it, talking badly and looking badly.Who is it? Rahi said.

"My brother will know he is one year ahead of us. I don't know. " Rita said.

"I do not see the back,I'll see you when I come back with breakfast.Looks so bad? " Mahesh said.

"Oh,He gets up and walks out.Look fast."Rahi said.

"Hey this Ashish and his three men." Looking back, Mahesh said.

"Do you recognize him?" Bansi said.

"Yes, he is older than me." Mahesh said.

"What kind of man is he?" Rita said.

"This Valsad MLA is the son of Suresh Desai.And this college was also built by Suresh Desai.Ashishand three man is terrified of me."Mahesh said.

"Frightened! I don't understand." Rahi said.

"Listen to the former." Mahesh said.

(Past 3)

"In the beginning, there is a party in the college.This Ashish is already doing this because of his father's power.So it's only a matter of time before my college started,Ashish and all his other siblings were teasing the girl.At that time, a girl was being harassed in the middle of college."Mahesh said and explains the story of the past.

"What's my item bomb!" Ashish said.

Jill, Samir, Harsh his friends.

"She is worried,What could be,We're worried too much."Jill said.

("I was standing there listening to everything, And waited for something bad to happen." Mahesh said.)

"Why are you so arrogant?"Samir said.

"Hey, brother, let me show you something, I'm having fun." Ashish said.

"Brothers, if there is nothing between them all, do not do it." Harsh said.

"Hey, you keep quiet, you are scared when you are.There is no need to be afraid of others if you are with me."Ashish said.Immediately Ashish touches the girl's cheek.

"That's what the college owner taught you.The girl looks goodSo bother immediately?"The girl said.

"We are ready, always." Jill said.

"You say go to the hotel,The three of us will be with you,Let's have fun."Samir said.

(Mahesh gets very angry.)

"Hey, come to the hotel,Even if you see our strength.We will be happy too."Ashish said.Near the ear, "or rap."

"I will call the police and let them in,Think of your father, self respect, you are at stake. " The girl said.

"If the police come,So I'll save. I am ready to marry her for two days and then get a divorce. " Ashish said.

"So we are beggars, stay thirsty!We want to have fun too, what can we do?" Samir said.

"Then I will give you a divorce." Ashish said.

From there the girl tries to escape. And Mahesh comes in front of the girl till Ashish goes to catch her.

"Oh, the hero must be ready." Ashish said.

"Which movie did you see, brother?You will be cut at home, brother."Samir said.

"Why did you bring a cutter?" Mahesh said.

"Come on, get out of here." Ashish said.

"You want to come forward with superstition,

The girl wants to run away in fear,

Don't know what's on your face,

But Mahesh Patel wants to wash your face."Mahesh said.

"Speak well, can I win well?" Ashish said.

"Who wins? I want to win."Mahesh looked at the girl and said.

"Ohh, Finally?" Samir said.

"Quiet, Samir, let me talk now.The move reached a win-lose.There are fights in this college, if you are win then girl is yous." Ashish said.

"This girl is nothing object, I just want to save. " Mahesh said.

"Then save." Ashish said.

"I will save her and send her home without harm." Mahesh said.

After all this talk, these people get into fights.Since Mahesh has a slightly stiff body, he falls heavily on these three. Harsh doesn't come in between because he doesn't like it at all.It so happens that Mahesh saves the girl.

"Seen doing this in college,So I will kill you in the middle of college in the same way."After saying this, Mahesh leaves.Mahesh explains all this to Suresh Desai by going to his house.

"Did my son do that?" Suresh Desai said."Yes, uncle, he used to take advantage of his college and harass other people and tease the girl." Mahesh said.

"I'll explain my son." Suresh said.

(Past 2Present 2)

"This is how I have answered it.So you don't have to be scared. " Mahesh said.

"Who's scared? Why were four people watching now? That was to know." Rahi said.

"These people won't do anything until I'm there." Mahesh said.

"But I have something to do." Rahi said.

"Meaning." Rita said.And the other two look at her.

"I mean, I really enjoy correcting people like that,The fun of being with a man after healing is something different.And I will do it. " Rahi said.

"What work do you want to die for?" Bansi said.

"I do not want to die.He looked at me,So he will improve and become like you, Mahesh." Rahi said.

"You speak in your mind, don't you? There will very danger." Rita said.

"I am just fine,I just need your help." Rahi said.

"There is no such help." Rita said.

"No, don't stop." Mahesh grabbed Rita's hand and said.

"But there is a lot of fear and risk involved." Rita said.

"We'll be annoyed." Bansi said.

"Improves,That is important.I have a game that improves." Rahi said.

"Yes,Let me explain later if there is any, I will go now.It's time for class."Mahesh said.

Why did Mahesh get in trouble for talking like this to Rahi? Rahi looks intently and tries to understand. What is on Rahi's mind, no one knows. Is the time good or bad? Time game played, Only time will tell what was wrong and what was right.

....

Part 4 : Rahi's love story

From there Mahesh leaves on the pretext of class, This is shocking.

"You know,What are you doing?" Bansi said.

"Absolutely,Did it matter if I talked to this Mahesh about another boy too?Only for this question mark." Rahi said.

"Yes,I felt a little. " Rita said.

"Well,So you just speaks to see this. " Bansi said.

"No,Not just for the sake of speaking.Take sometime, i will revenge,It is a crime to think badly.Four people scared of Mahesh.I will take advantage of it.I just need your help.Trust me i'll be Mahesh's,Don't be like anyone else.The way a little bit loves me,So i love your brother.Play game, Mahesh doesn't know that. He must love me,So much for me.He must have been happy to see me.This will change a lotand I will tell him in due course that I love you too." Rahi said.

"Oh,So you both love each other,But both can't say right now. " Rita said.

"Oh, I can do itbut not now.Just game right now,Don't let him know.This game will awaken Mahesh's love more,If he looks at me, he will learn a lesson.And Ashish and his siblings improved a lot too.Maybe he won't look down on anyone in the future." Rahi said.

"Well, if that's the case." Rita said.

"I do not think so.Also try. If it doesn't get better, it will stay away from us." Rahi said.

"That's right." Bansi said.

"What's on your mind?" Rita said.

"You both tell Mahesh that I want to meet Ashish,And slowly I started to like it." Rahi said.

"You're going to waste of time, I think so. " Rita said.

"Nothing will happen,If you just wait for result. Now you go. I'm going too." Rahi said.

After all this talk, Rita and Bansi leave. Immediately Rahi leaves her bag with a piece of paper on the table, Which Rita sees. Suddenly a boy comes, Whose mouth is covered with a handkerchief, The eyes are fitted with goggles, The hat is worn over the head. He came wearing a black coat, The man sits at the table, holds the letter, reads it.

"Who is this? Something is wrong!"Rita sees all this and thinks. Since the mouth is not visible, Rita falls into superstition and this confusion of Rahi makes me think.

Who reads Rahi's letter? And as soon as he gets out of college.Rita chases after him. But he doesn't get it, runs away.

"What would Rahi have written in the letter?Not now but later I will catch and ask.It doesn't work to deceive my brother.She will play a game with Ashish but he will never play a game with my brother.I'll just hold it.Rahi's game in her way and my superstition in my way.Come on in, take a look and enjoy yourself!Game is start."Rita thinks in her mind.

Then Rita goes to her class, It is thought, So Rahi and Bansi call her.

"What do you think?I'm doing well.I don't think anything bad for Mahesh."Rahi said.

"Yes, yes, I know, you don't think badly.I was feeling a little superstitious inside. Maybe there's nothing wrong with doing good! " Rita said.

"Don't think too much,Rahi also loves Mahesh, it will be good.Don't force your brain to think like this. " Bansi said.

"Yes, just don't think.Now you think. " Rita said.

("The idea is not this Bansi. Rahi hides something big from us. Asking Mahesh to love, he reads the letter again. I'll just find out and jump. " Rita thinks in her mind.)

"Rita,Let me tell you something. In the future I will be someone's, So simply Mahesh." Rahe said.

"Yes, yes, nothing. Let's do our study." Rita said.

("Probably seen my men, Otherwise, I have never seen Rita like this. " Rahi thinks in her mind.)

("Words create magic. I just want to recognize that magic.You are not visible. " Rita thinks in her mind.)

("I do not think so badly. I love Mahesh, The letter taker cannot be brought out right now. I think you're just looking at it and thinking. Time will tell who he is. If I have to release Mahesh for that, I will do it first. " Rahi thinks in his mind.)

"Don't forget to go home or go out of college and tell all game Mahesh to do that much now." Rahi says to Rita.

"Yes, yes, I will say that by going out now." Rita said.

After all this, the class ends in a short time. All are coming out on different routes. Rita Mahesh joins, Rahi separates and Bansi separates. It happens that Rahi is leaving the college, Then Ashish is sitting there all together. Looks bad, And all his siblings are talking.

"It's difficult to talk as far as Mahesh is concerned." Ashish said.

"Only when Mahesh has to do something before he can say no." Samir said.

"Kill Mahesh and make you disappear." Jill said.

"I worked hard a few days ago, You are the one who is fight.Nothing matches the big fight.Ashish gets a clean heart, not lust." Harsh said.

"Don't spoke." Ashish said.

"Brother, keep your mind and pure heart with you.I had heard that one in two or four good men turned out to be a bad one.But this is going to get worse. " Jill said.

"It's not like I'll be with you when the time comes.But you have to have time to do something.Don't hit the line anywhere.She is also someone's daughter, If you ask Mahesh to kill him, he is also someone's son."Harsh said.

"We are also someone's son."Jill said.

"Well, I can see,We'll catch up when we get a chance to do it later.Just wait now.Mahesh and his sister come,So let's go."Sameer sees Mahesh and his sister coming and said.

These people go out in a hurry, Rita tries to tell her brother to do what Rahi has said.

"These people run away when they see,It would have been better." Mahesh said.

"I don't know if it improves or not.I have one thing to say to you. " Rita said.

"Yeah tell me, what happened?" Maheshsaid.

"Nothing happened, but one thing is for sure." Rita said.

"Why is it slow to talk so fast?" Mahesh said.

"Rahi wants to meet Ashish." Rita said.

"What are you talking about!" Mahesh is surprised.

"Yes, she wants to be friends with Ashish, she wants to move on." Rita said.

"But how can she do such a thing?" Mahesh said.

"I do not know.All I have to say is that as long as you live around it she will not be able to find Ashish. " Rita said.

"Why is this Rahi doing this?" Mahesh said.

"She asked to see you tomorrow.You can help her, no one else can,she said." Rita said.

"I'll see her tomorrow alone. Listen to what she has to say.Why are you doing this?" Mahesh said.

He gets out of his car and thinks of driving.

("Rahi wants to do the last thing. Why does Ashish do this even though he knows it is bad? I kept thinking about it and I fell in love with it.It doesn't matter if he says to go with another, but why with Ashish?Rahi does this even though I save it so well. You do not understand at all. Today, for the first time, I got in trouble with you. Maybe you never thought of me, And I never left,So you feel like I have nothing in mind, But you are in my heart and mind and you will be.What do you do for a living and what do you need? I don't think any of this, If this is your happiness then that's fine.

All I have to say is,

Was it necessary to leave?

If you don't like it, why not?

But I needed to understand.

Grief arises,

Not trying to stand up at all,

Sometimes I have to say,

And the time for tears has come.

Would have tried before,

So i'm happy today

But by no means saying,

What does she want without knowing?

Just know today,

And then the sacrifice of my heart is for you,

I don't think so. Now all of a sudden I feel like I've come down." Mahesh thinks in his mind.)

"What do you think, Mahesh?" Rita said.

"I don't think so." Mahesh said.

("Mahesh is in pain but can't say. Rahi also called stone heart, She is doing this even though she knows that my brother will suffer so much. Let me see you tomorrow." Rita thinks in her mind.)

"Truth be told, trouble happens!" Rita said.

"Yes,The problem is getting worse.Why does Rahi do this?She may not know that I have a passion for it.There is a feeling for that. I'm afraid of losing it.Maybe I didn't say it was wrong.I had to tell her.That's my mistake. " Mahesh said.

"Time will tell.But I didn't know a thing."After this, Rita, who had seen a man in the canteen, takes a letter and tells all the answers.

"Someone new came.Now we have to work on having fun.Rahi's telling you this, man with letter, affection for Ashish, it will be a lot of fun to solve this puzzle. Gradually a new man also came.Not a little, but a big scandal.We have to wait and see what Rahi will talk about tomorrow.Just look now, Rahi, you are misleading me.Maybe that's true, I don't even know if I love her." Mahesh said.

....

Part : 5 Start Game, wait and watch.

The next day, the four meet in the canteen. (Rahi, Mahesh, Rita, Bansi.)

"Hey, I told him what you said." Rita said.

"Yes, listen to what I was saying, Mahesh.Ashish can't even talk to me as long as you are Mahesh. Then," said Rahi.

"So I say stay away from you?" Mahesh said.

"Listen carefully.This is what has created fear in their minds, because of that fear they just look at me.I want to meet and it looks great. " Rahi said.

Mahesh is sitting in front of his sister as if thinking a little.

"Then something may happen that you go with him,And say that Rahi wants to talk to you. " Rahi said.

"Why are you doing this?" I don't understand anything." Mahesh said.

"The time will come when it will be understood,What more can I ask for now? In the end, everything will be fine. " Rahi said.

("She is waiting answer for me and says everything will be fine." Mahesh thinks in his mind.)

"Where did you suddenly get lost, Mahesh?" Rahi said.

"Oh no, I was just thinking, let me know what you want to do,I can't answer without knowing. " Mahesh said.

"The truth is, I like Ashish a little bit. Then I will be like that.I have to live with someone after we all get college leave from time to time,So I thought so.You explain your way to AshishAnd you says if he tries to talk to me, the girl will never start talking, the boy will have to try.You explain it and talk.What happens next? " Rahi said.

"Everything is thought and spoken, right? Then nothing will happen!" Bansi said.

"Yes, that's right. Nothing should happen then. " Rita said.

"Let nothing happen, have faith.Mahesh, everything will be fine. I have taken action now that I understand who is in trouble. " Rahi said.

"Never mind, I'm going with Ashish.Let me tell you what happened." Mahesh said.

Mahesh leaves and these three talk.

"Rahi, you really take my brother!" Rita said.

"Oh no, I will tell him before the end of six months. I love him.Believe me, don't let Mahesh spoil you.They must have been thinking of doing bad things with as many girls as I did.Looks good, it's not the girl's fault.These people have a bad understanding,Tease these guys just by looking at any girl.When teasing occurs, only one thing runs through the girl's mind ('Maybe if this does something wrong with me, I will not go home, I will not let my parents' honor be harmed.') This is the same thought that confused away at girls every day they come to this college.But what can the girls do who jumps on boy's dad's power at the same time and saves the girl who comes in between these people.But Mahesh has given a strong answer.So I'm willing to sacrifice alone, not for myself but for every girl like me, And history will be with me as proof. The answer is yes, I will tell Ashish and the whole world,No one will get bad idea but if the time given has improved then the world will be waiting for you. Your thoughts will be waiting and these are the thoughts I am going to give to the world. If you don't help I'll do it alone, But in this college and also in other colleges, when someone wakes up and responds verbally to correct the boy, these people will know about a girl and her house. Only then will I be very happy inside, I didn't think much about my house before doing this, I just thought Nirbhaya case,Nine month old girl, Doctor's rap, Then the rap-taking advantage of such a national politics chair, In this, everyone's house cried for the rest of their lives. And with my help, if any house survives, I will do and will continue to do. This is the culture of India I will try to improve till my last breath because the soul of all the raped girls is with me, I don't care if you don't stay. If I start the game, I will finish for them, I will show the world what is wrong and what is true, just change the idea, a lot will change." Rahi said.

"So, Your idea is best, Rahi i proud of you" Bansi said.

"The idea is that I have done well. Nowadays, I am told badly that I am betraying Mahesh.So I do not betray, I betray the bad society.An era of reform is also needed.This will spread as soon as my words happen.It is up to you to help or not to help.I just want an answer from these people to do wrong and this is my right which even the government will not stop me and you will not stop me for your brother.If it goes wrong, the responsibility will be mine and if it goes well, we will all be responsible.If we continue, gradually everyone will join and even if they don't join, there will be no problem. " Rahi said sadly.

"If you have such a good idea, I will hand it over to you, my brother. Whatever you have to do with my brother, I am ready. " Rita said.

"Thank you so much." Rahi said happily.

Mahesh finds Ashish in college till then and he appears in the parking lot. People who don't want to improve look bad on all girls. That is why Ashish and all his other friends get frightened when they see Mahesh walking with them, Ashish and Ashish's friend fear them.

"When will you people improve?" Mahesh said.

"What's your problem,We are fine. " Samir said.

"Whatever it is, Rahi wants to meet you." Mahesh said.Then Ashish is surprised.

"I do not know. What you are say?" Ashish said.

"To be honest,One thing you have to believe is that I will meet you. " Mahesh said.

"Yes, what do you want to believe?" Ashish said.

"Meet Rahi and you too will be like that forever. Rahi is very good. You think badly of the other girls and her but you have to improve and live for her all your life. You have to live with someone for the rest of our lives, so let's live well. " Mahesh said.

"Yes, I will do as you wish and as Rahi wish." Ashish said.

"Yes, I'm leaving now. I'll call and tell you where to meet. Give me the number." Maheshsaid.

Mahesh keeps taking the numberand go outside. Then these people talk inside.

"Why is this happening today?" Ashish said.

"I think something else." Jillsaid.

"Not only you but me too. What could be? " Ashish said.

"Brother, whatever it is, if we get together, we will gradually find out what really happens." Harsh said.

"Don't take revenge!" Ashish said.

"I understand.If you look away, you will know.The first thing is what she wants to doAnd if there is a good thing at all, it can be the same -If a boy crosses the line and the girl sees a little strength in the boy, then he gets fed up.If there is something like that, it will start letting you know in a few days. And we're just passing the time.So something like this passes your time.What's wrong with that, too?If there is nothing to kill, the answer will be found." Harsh said.

"This is the first time you've ever thought of us." Ashish said.

"It simply came to our notice then,The difference is that right now you like what I'm saying.And there is nothing wrong with that.There is nothing better for you than this, and if it is true you will be judged. " Harsh said.

"And if something goes wrong!" Ashishsaid.

"Then you believe me,Whatever happens, maybe something bad happenedSo I will tell you what will be the way for these people to go to heaven. " Harsh said.

"We people are brainwashed into hitting the lines,But then you will think terrible. " Ashish said.

"You brainstorm and your time,Let's try to figure out what this game is all about.

Many would have been kings,

Many will be killed,

There will be a lot of trouble,

So there will be a lot of jokes.

If only they had found a way to make fun of them,That day will be his last days."Speaking like this, Ashish will be a little and immediately looks with an angry look.

So on this side of the canteen, suddenly someone's call rings on Rahi's phone.

"Hey, the phone rang. Let's talk." Rahi picks up the phone and goes out.

Rita immediately wonders who is the one on the phone for which she had to stay and go out, chases and listens on the phone.

"Hey, I wanted to tell you, I'll call you, not you. And how is everything going?But remember that I am with you in case of any problem.I'll call you later when I'm leaving. " Saying this, she puts down the phone and Rita stands behind her.

"Who was on the phone?" Rita said.

"Oh no, nothing else." Rahi said.

"You were hiding something. Who was the phone call man?" Rita said.

"Ok ok, but don't tell anyone." Rahi said.

Rahi tells Rita that everything will be known in time. (One more story.)

. . . .
. . . .

Part : 6 Rahi and Ashish meet

Rahi and Mahesh talk while walking in college.

"I will call Ashish when you say so." Mahesh said.

"Yes, you should, but she should come alone." Rahi said.

"Then you go to the canteen and he will come." Mahesh said.

Rahi goes to the canteen.She is sitting. After a while Ashish is seen coming and he comes and talks to Rahi.

"Can I sit down?" Ashish said.

"Yes, yes, why not, sit here." Rahisaid.

"You told Mahesh something about me!" Ashish said.

"Yes, that's why I called you." Rahi said.

"So what was the point?" Ashish said.

"Something like this is happening,You were looking at me in the canteen that day, I was fascinated by your strength.Then Mahesh would say something before you had a fight,So I thought so you want to talk to me but don't try to come with me because of Mahesh.So I thought I told Mahesh to call you,Let's settle everything and start anew.Such quarrels will never end.I thought something good would happen if we both became friends.Everyone stays together and has fun.It is possible to move forward slowly."Rahi said.

"Next, so I don't understand!" Ashish said.

"Why don't you understand? I have to explain!"Rahi said.

"It was the first time had ever called a girl,So the brain is dizzy,That is why nothing is understood and cannot be understood. " Ashish said.

"All that happen, Talk to you soon and keep up the good content. " Rahi said.

"I didn't ask, what will you take? Tea or coffee?" Ashish said.

"Coffee."Rahi said.

("She asked for it right away without embarrassment." Ashish thinks in his mind.)

"What do you think?" I'm just sitting here. Bring me some coffee. " Rahi said.

"Yes, bring it." Ashish said.

(Then Ashish thinks while having coffee."Problemso don't look.She like a good thing.The rest of the girls are hard to identify.If Rahi is doing something thinking, then she is not thinking anything.But why do I think I have the opportunity to take it." Ashish thinks in his mind.)

Then he goes back to having coffee.In this way, they both get into a talk and Mahesh sees from a distance and gives himself trouble.If by mistake Rahi's eye falls on Mahesh then Mahesh starts running away from there.After talking for a while, the two of them shake hands and go away with their siblings. Rahi meets her people.

"What,How do you feel about that? " Bansi said.

"I felt a strange man. Agar will fall. He thinks a lot." Rahi said.

"Nothing, everything will happen slowly. Mahesh, what do you think? " Rita said.

"It's simply lot happen, Whatever Rahi wants will happen. But you need to be careful. " Mahesh said.

"I don't think so." Rahi said.

On the other hand, Ashish reached with his friends.

"What, how was the first meeting?" Samir said.

"I don't think there's anything wrong with that. Things are the same." Ashish said.

"Then why do you think so much?" Harsh said.

"I things first meeting is very funny completed but confusion high level. It's all about friendship now. " Ashish said.

"So let's talk, if anything happens we're all here." Harsh said.

"Brother, keep your mind on everything, even if we are like Stranger, but your mind should be on." Ashish grabs Harsh's shoulder and speaks.

"You don't take any tension, I'll keep an eye on you, there will be no problem at all, I will keep pointing at you." Harsh said.

"Thank you." Ashish said.

"What did you say?" This is the first time such words have come out of your mouth!" Harsh said.

"I think this girl will be correcting you?" Samir said.

" Why do you have good words for it? We just look at the girl with lustful eyes. We are not going to improve and I do not want to improve. The only answer I can give you is to have fun, I'm not going to get better. " Ashish said.

"But do you remember Mahesh's talk?" Harsh said.

"Now that man is shaking me." Ashish said.

"I do not know. What happens to you is good. It is not good to live with sin in mind. " Harsh said.

"I am just a bad person. Bloodshed, rap, fights make my name shine. I don't know anything else. " Ashish said angrily.

"You didn't think about it when you were in the canteen, why you didn't remember the night, why you didn't want to use her body, why you didn't want to say bad things about her then, or why you were there." Shut up Brother, your brain is used now. Until now, only you thought that everything would go wrong, but today, for the first time, you have gone to meet someone with respect. You are in the mode of change today. You just have to be more discriminating with the help you render toward other people." Harsh said.

"You gave a good speech but I never changed." After saying this, Ashish takes the bike and runs away in anger.

"My brother has a few bites. Gradually, it will get better." Samir said.

"If it improves, never remind him,That's how we all get annoyed. We have to give him time to be alone. If it's good, let it be. " Harsh said. "But what I didn't expect happens." Jill said.

"Times change. If it is beyond comprehension, sometimes life is hectic and sometimes there is an atmosphere of peace. In the meantime, Ashish is completely depressed today. It will be fun, but this time it will be fun to change something." Harsh said.

After a while, that day of college is about to end. So at that time Ashish is sitting outside like a lurker wearing vulgar clothes, at that time Ashish changes from his fun and immediately calms down. Ashish's seems to be coming from opposite Rahi. Then Ashish's brothers understand and go away.

"Is this all gone!" Rahi said.

"Blood is made from bones, bones are not made of blood. If you keep going, there will be some blood in the bones! " Ashish said.

"What you say? Anyway,You don't like sitting in class? You are wandering. " Rahi said.

"Who sits in the class. Let's get through. " Ashish said.

"And what company are these clothes wearing? If someone wears such clothes! Come to a few professionals. You are the son of MLA. Come out of this world for a while. In this way, sitting in the corner, you just get the name recognition and nothing else. You just have to be more discriminating with the help you render toward other people." Rahi said.

"I do not want anything to come. You guys stay educated I'm fine. And yes, I will try to change, please. " Ashish said.

"Change your life style. Many things change nowadays. Think from the heart whether you really are right or do not want to be right. A name will not get you anything, but making a name for yourself will make the world yours. " Rahi said. After saying so much, Ashish gets another answer and runs away.

It's okay to run away, but the next day the whole thing changes. Everyone looks at him as if he had come to a college class for the first time. The whole face also changes. The hair is neatly cut and the clothes come as Rahi said. Then things change slowly. Since Rahi and Mahesh are not together, sometimes Mahesh bring tears from their eyes at home. Seeing Rahi with Ashish, Mahesh gets in trouble but since Mahesh really loves, he stays in Rahi's happiness.

....

Part 7 : The fact of Rahi

It's been a while now. Then in a few days his last year's farewell party is planned. He calls Rahi, Mahesh Rita and Bansi in the canteen on the morning of the farewell party.

"Why did you call us all of a sudden?" Rita said.

"The time is up. Ashish has changed completely. " Rahi said.

"Then stay with him." Mahesh said.

"You're angry with me!" Rahi said seeing Mahesh's anger.

"Do you realize how bad that man was?" Mahesh said.

"Everything is conscious and I took that step just thinking." Rahi said.

"No one else came to your notice. He took the name with me and I will try to change it. Then dream of living with him! " Mahesh said.

"You have the right to speak. Then give you a lightning bolt. " Rahi said.

"Why are you a DP's power, you will give me a tweak! You were with Ashish, that's the big tweak for me. What happened to Ashish? " Mahesh said.

"Game over." Rahi said.

Mahesh is completely shocked.

"Game means Ashish! I don't understand?" Mahesh said.

So let the whole thing tell him.

"That means you play with Ashish!" Mahesh said.

"To fix it and It was a small revenge to think badly of me. And it will save a lot." Rahi said.

"You are right." Mahesh said.

"The problem is, he doesn't know it yet, and when it does, you'll be ready to save me." Rahi said.

"Oh, I will save you." Mahesh said.

"One problem is another. Today, he has organized a Shimla picnic for four of us and all four of us. I'm leaving tonight. " Rahi said.

"So what do we do?" Rita said.

"Ok to go. He doesn't know anything yet." Rahi said.

"Come on, let's not let anything happen to me. "Mahesh said.

"So I'm ready to go." Rahi said.

"It's not a problem to go!" Bansi said.

"Yes, but Mahesh I know you love me." Rahi said.

"Yes son." Mahesh said.

"If you want to face someone, be ready, but be afraid to talk. Let me just say, I love you. " Rahi said. Mahesh is ashamed.

"Me too." Mahesh said.

'This is how the two get together which Ashish does not even know. After finishing the farewell party at night, he came home that day and told me everything every day.

(Past 1 present 1)

4 March 2020

Everyone is sitting at home and listening to Jatin.

"I didn't think it was enough that everyone left for Shimla that night, but that night I found out that Mahesh was dead. So it is not known whether these people left Shimla or not. The phone doesn't ring. We were all terrified. A postmortem of Mahesh the next morning revealed that Light Belladonna had been poisoned and that the effects had spread within seven to eight hours. In other words, if Mahesh is killed by giving poison, then Rita will not go for picnic. Then the next day a call came from Shimla that Rahi was not seen in the hotel." Jatin said.

"Then all suspicion goes there, why didn't the police do anything?" Said Satish.

"ML is his son. No police can touch him without proof." Jatin said.

"So Rahi may have been taken to Shimla or drama?" Satish said.

"The house also has bear steps and rahi blood. These people have done something from there. " Jatin said.

"So didn't you call her either Rita or Bansi?" Satish said.

"She didn't call anyone on the way out, nobody knew about it or let her know." Jatin said.

"Can I say something?" Ravi said.

"Did you keep my son safe?" Jatin said.

"Yes, that's right, Dad." Satish said.

"Yes, son of a speak." Jatin said.

"I have three questions in my mind." Ravi said.

"Maybe we can get some answer in your talk. " Jatin said.

"The answer is no,

The question is the first one to which Rahi gave a letter.

Question second : While playing another Rahi game, he hid Mahesh's talk and talked to Ashish, but no one but him knew this? Finally!

Question third: When she go out of the house for picnics, no one calls by name and that is the answer to these questions. Rahi did not leave without calling. Only one call it's proof but they can't. how?" Ravi said.

"Someone called the record not checked." Jatin said.

"You see it, I see what I see." Ravi said.

"Is there any other man among these people?" Jatin said.

"Yes, it's one hundred percent." Ravi said.

"Can there be any way?" Jatin said.

"As you said, if someone has given poison, not seven or eight hours ago. If so many hours ago And at night when Mahesh dead has given poison at three or four o'clock because his dead time nine o'clock something, 3 o'clock the party has started. It's confusion only things 3 o'clock party start then who gave poison mahesh? it's internal peson!" Ravi said. "So let's ask the canteen waiter." Satish said.

"There is no answer. If there is a waiter, then the owner of the canteen also works under Suresh Desai. Suresh will save his son. That is why the man is oppressed. " Ravi said.

"Then the answer will never be found." Satish said.

"The answer will be found, brother. But when we don't show our faces. " Ravi said.

"What do you get for not showing your face?" Jatin said.

"Even the police don't know who we are by not showing their faces. Satish is going to take advantage of this. The two of us will get together and confuse them as they confuse us in the way we keep our game behind them." Ravi said.

"I can't understand." Satish said.

"What's going on in your mind is really strong. Explain to us what you want to do." Jatin said.

"Even if we get these people out, these people will get out on the power of the father MLA. I'm looking forward to it. " Ravi said.

"In this, I have lost my daughter. Let no one else lose." Jatin said.

"No one can be lost. Listen to me done who is in the canteen, who called Rahi, has already poisoned Mahesh as the effect starts after 8 hours of light belladonna poison.

These people have meet for a picnic on the way home when he may have fallen ill. And the big thing is that there is no bus or travels and no such train to Shimla in one night."Ravi said.

"You mean, they didn't go to Shimla." Satish said.

"It is also true that those people have not gone to Shimla one hundred percent and Rahi has not gone one hundred percent. What Rahi has done here is still there, but I can't get it." Ravi said.

"It seems to be true, nothing like Shimla can be reached. I didn't even think about it, and it never crossed my mind! " Jatin said.

"No, Heavily planned then work successfully, Someone played a big game. Ashish may know that Mahesh and Rahi will be joining later. Ashish already knows that. Then it may have happened that on the day of going for a picnic, Rahi has been kept somewhere. Rahi is unknown at this time what he will do after leaving the situation." Ravi said.

"If those people didn't get there the next day, then why did they get Rahi's blood the next day?" Satish said.

"Who said they didn't arrive the next day? They must have arrived Shimla the next day." Ravi said.

"Then how can that be?" Jatin said.

"Show them if book a bus or train ticket, or get some travel details?" Ravi said.

"Didn't you notice anything like that?" Jatin said.

Ravi will be slowly smile.

"Why are you smiling?" Satish said.

"These people have also bought the police. Otherwise he checks the ticket first. But he did not take it seriously." Ravi said.

"You mean Nikhil too!" Jatin said.

"Yes, Nikhil, those people have already done what Rahi has to do. If they have already taken a ticket from Surat airport to Delhi as per the plan, it will be four or five hours after going to Delhi." Ravi said.

"Your brain is strong, you will hold on to all the moves." Jatin said.

"I have been winning in the game of chess, the only difference is that this time my vizier is alive and his whole army. I have to grasp each one carefully. Even without fear. These people have kept the magic very strong but I will strike directly at Raja. All will be found without proof and when found, I will kill them by playing like their game. I don't know another thing, if Rahi was telling you everything, then who gave the letter? " Ravi said.

"No, She didn't tell us anything." Jatin said.

"I will hold on to whatever it is." Ravi said.

"Your brain is racing, but we don't think so." Jatin said.

"The reason you don't like that idea is because you kept her grief going, if you get out of that grief you will get an answer. Assuming that I consider Satish a brother and you family too, my mind is still talking about you. I am a player who, with a little brainstorming in the way those people played the game, can tell what happened. This is how I get to the point where they start. Rahi's sacrifice should not be in vain. They also have to answer, that a girl who was ready to fight alone to solve all the problems in college by thinking of everything well, then what happened that Rita Mahesh and Bansi had to go away. The only reason for this is that Ashish has got his own arrogance who has not even thought of a single life to answer him by playing a game with him to think well. Life and life is a word but for me it is different. Life is the whole life and life is the way of life. Life is for someone who dies every day, but life is lived by those who move forward with true hope. The rest is no different. Many have come like this Ashish, if you don't finish my life from scratch, then my name is not Ravi either. I will found all game." Ravi said.

"But somehow you will do all this." Jatin said.

"Reverse situation then action on time.

You must have been sitting on a swinging seat.

There will be a school run in childhood,

Mathematical examples will also be taught,

But she remained trapped in the riddle of life.

A lot has happened or not met,

Not to be outdone, waiting to be answered,

There is a lot to gain but no strength to lose,

Rahi who came with a life of two moments,

I will make your life immortal.

What word should I use for you,

So you have sacrificed for the girl,

The thing is, not even the idea of family,

After that it was a matter of pressure,

Left you what happened,

I also understand the game of the one who bites you.

I was probably someone's brother,

But Rahi, you call me brother,

I'll go to work and finish

The responsibility of that work will be yours, yes it will be yours. But this time, you will be responsible for the destruction of Satan, not for the wrong, and I am ready to be the cause. Yes, I am ready to fight. It will be my responsibility to do justice, and not stop me from doing this. I am not one of you, so no one will doubt me. " Ravi said.

"Are you ready to do so much for us?" Jatin said. "Soon I will bite those people and I will deceive them in the lot game, even without anyone's power. Because wherever

Rahi is, her faith and prayers for me will be with me." Ravi said.

"Yes, son, we are with you." Jatin said.

There, Ravi suddenly looks at a photo on a wall.

"Whose photo is this?" Ravi said.

"This is a photo of a swindler living in our house." Jatin said.

"But there is a necklace on the photo." Ravi said.

"I don't know if he is alive or dead, but he is not alive for us. Don't ask about it, son. "Jatin said.

"Yes, nothing. My brain will continue. You go to bed without any tension. It's like a little night. Satish and I should go out for a while. " Ravi said.

"Yes, nothing. My brain will continue. You go to bed without any tension. It's like a little night. Satish and I should go out for a while. " Ravi said.

"Yes, go but don't go too far, it's night time." Jatin said.

"I'm just going to keep Satish calm. He loves Rahi very much, he can't cry. " Ravi said. Then Ravi and Satish go out. Jatin and his other family members talk inside.

"His brain is huge, he is sitting thinking somewhere!" Jayesh said.

"Yes Dad, he spoke hard and I think this Ravi will be looking for a reason." Jatin said.

"Satish has taken care of the lion, now he will roar and attack the other person's house. Today, I feel the last hope. " Reshma said.

"This will not even give anyone time to think and the director will do it again. Everything will have to find a reason. God hears us. He has sent us a man against whom even the best player seems to work. But don't know why this poor man was? " Jatin said.

"Satish used to say that there was orphan in his house, so Satish saved him. After that, if there is such a nature, then we started living in peace." Reshma said.

"It's just a matter of having fun, now we'll find the answer. " Jatin said.

[Satish was in a lot of trouble, what can be done? When Satish himself was broken, someone had to agitate to get rid of the worms of the society. Ravi has come, now the answer was yet to be found.]

....

Part 8 Ravi's talk

What a day it would be, when a brother would say, 'I was not here, and what happened to my Ben in the circle of not being mine.' What would Satish be feeling, what would have happened knowing what happened, what happened to Ben that no one would have even thought of. What kind of people have fallen in the society or this society can be said to be the culprit of those who are jumping on their breath? Maybe today is the magic of life in which people of ordinary family are living under oppression.

Ravi takes Satish out, after night time Ravi starts talking to Satish. But since Satish is in a lot of trouble, he cannot speak. Both of them are sitting at the table with the tea.

"Satish, oy Satish, say something, man." Ravi said.

But Satish looks in front of him and then back at the table.

"Brother, once you trust me, I will do everything as before." Ravi said.

"Like before, will I bring Rahi back?" Satish said. Ravi doesn't say anything.

"She is three years younger than me. I haven't seen her for the last four years. She haven't seen her for four years. I kept it in my heart, it's true that Dad is our Jatin but I saved him a lot. " Satish said.

"Do one thing, you are close to Daman. All the problems will go away and I will be able to sit alone and understand the whole game. " Ravi said.

Then he takes Satish to Daman. Ravi goes to Daman and drinks hard liquor and after the drink is full, Ravi sees tears slowly coming out of Satish's eyes. He holds her hand lightly and then looks at her and speaks.

"Satish, if you have a brother, it is our obligation to move forward even after suffering badly." Ravi said.

"But my family is being punished for something. The only difference is that if we think well of everything, we have to make a full sacrifice!" Satish said angrily.

"Brother, this is not something that is visible. Rahi is not that soon started the game. Rahi is still hiding something. Ashish may have said something about Rahi that we can't talk about. The first and last thing is that if so many people are spoiled, it will not get better in a few days."Ravi said.

"So Ashish pretended to improve?" Satish said.

"Yes, Brightness is the play of improving. All had met his people and he was probably waiting for Rahi to do something wrong. And then Rahi must have known that we don't care Because we will find out only when these people have taken Rahi away from somewhere. "Ravi said.

"You drop my drink." Satish said.

"Take another, but today the matter will be settled and I will start working from tomorrow." Ravi said. "But I still don't understand one thing. If Rahi had said that she would have loved Mahesh, Mahesh would have helped her and taken care of her." Satish said.

"Keep Rahi in a separate place. Rita is Mahesh's sister, if your sister is left, what will she do when she sees you in trouble? " Ravi said.

"Trouble will calm you down after asking." Satish said.

"Rita must have told her brother everything just to calm him down." Ravi said.

"But he was crying at his house, said Rahi to Dad." Satish said.

"Understand one thing carefully, that Rita has told Rahi that Mahesh is crying. So what was Mahesh Rowe doing there? I don't know if she understood. All that is known is that Mahesh cried. I don't think so, and if I think of another point, Rita said it is because he sees both fear and risk. " Ravi said.

"If she had said that, Mahesh would not have turned around, paying attention to him. Whatever it was, Rita would have told him by talking." Satish said.

"Yes, now you slowly understand everything. The second po int may be that Mahesh went to tell Ashish for the first time, He may have said the same thing to Ashish or later, If he gets in trouble, there is no one worse than me. If he meets Ashish, he has said only to improve. There is no problem. That's point noted." Ravi said.

"Why does your brain run in such a predicament?" Satish said.

"It will be a big problem for you in the face of the loss of my whole family, but for me, cut the heart. And a whole broken heart for you. " Ravi said. "I can understand your plight. But first explain to me that you say that if Ashish knows everything then why he doesn't do anything at the same time? " Satish said.

"First you thought, why did Rahi know whatever Ashish was thinking? Uncle said everything that Ashish was thinking at that time. Hey, do you know what is going on in someone's mind? Say? " Ravi said.

"You really think you don't know. How could Rahi know that? " Satish said.

"Ashish used to do this in front of Rahi, explaining to all the brothers and sisters to do it, which makes it seem as if everything we do changes. But he would deliberately show it in front of Rahi so that it seems that Rahi is doing what is right and good. " Ravi said. "Oh, I mean the whole thing is clear. Rahi was playing but another game was being played on it, which is not visible to anyone. And that's what you want to catch. " Satish said.

"I want to capture the whole story. Right now I'm totally unaware, just trying to figure out what's perfect, they're far ahead of us, we just have to overtake and overtake them. It would not have been so easy if Rahi had gone, so the whole thing has to go from the last to the first. It needs to be caught." Ravi said.

"Is there anyone else in this game?" Satish said.

"Yes." Ravi said.

"Dad used to say that Harsh could be so weird?" Satish said.

"Not at all, It is simply brought between a man to leave an illusion in front of us. Harsh is the cause but the game is played by someone else. After using so much brain, What do you think! Harsh may have been shown in front of a character asking to speak simply. The reason is simply that if we sit down to think about everything, there is a man at that point, You can never catch it. That is why it has been deliberately brought out. There is no Harsh. " Ravi said.

"Brother, nothing comes to my mind all day long and whatever came up came going. Now bring another. " Satish said.

"As I continue to talk to you, new ideas will not come to mind and will stop." Ravi said.

"But why do you think I'm depress? What could a similar drinker do? " Satish said.

"Appears in front, Not at all,

Not understandable

There is no living environment,

There is no such thing as an easy night out.

People playing on the field have fun,

Some people are jealous of it, Having fun is just a joke,

Fear is the thing that stays with us while digging.

The talk of love becomes a joke as the days go by,

So no one understands this,

There are so many in this world,

But if the day is good then the man sitting in front is ours.

I don't trust myself because this is the body,

Do not hesitate to betray your own body,

Cancer Blood pressure Diabetes is a lot for the body,

Then such people slowly poison!

The poison that covers the mouth from the front is just a thing of the past for these people,

So what about living in a small situation?

Take special care of the family together,

But what of the outward wrong?

Now for the fun of watching Ramayana Mahabharata,

Did you learn?

Listening to diarrhea,

Got it?

Good talk

What in life?

Talk to someone quietly

But what if we are not calm?

There is so much to gain in this world,

What if there is strength?

There is nothing wrong with that, ask him

Who deceived and martyred his boys,

What if there is no strength from the front?

Annoyingly Libran - always rational, easily hurt emotionally, very passionate and maybe a little too intense.

Talk to you soon and keep up the good content.

No matter how many we are,

Everyone is going to study,

Don't think about what will happen while having fun,

Did everything Rahi,

But not the idea of his compulsion.

Last year in four and three,

Don't think about it in the middle of the year.

It's just that the time has come to fight against time, there is no need to pay, it will only happen when you are with me in my game. I will not come out in the same way Ashish hides someone. In the same way you have to hide me from King. I have to hide to know their whole story. And almost I will see other people too. The wait may not be over. You just have to be more discriminating with the help you render toward other people." Ravi said.

"Everything went really wet." Satish said.

"You don't wear anything, now all I have to do is look." Ravi said.

"Your age seven to ten year, What was eaten! I want to eat." Satish said.

"Leave it all, tell me now that you will be with me in all work?" Ravi said.

"Yes, yes, why not? I am with you everywhere. You are the real man for my house. What you can't do, you have to do. And you have never thought of doing that and the family is not yours, even though all this is my right. " Satish said.

"Now he has kept me. Like brother, I owe you a great debt which was to be paid when the time came and now is the time, To pay favors. If you keep me well, I will give a good answer in return. This will be my biggest battle in the world and you will be my wazeer. 'Let's checkmate' just the two of us. It's too late now. " Ravi said.

What will be the answer for these two people who are looking for a big reason? Will he be able to take the next step? Will the whole situation give way to life? The only thing left to do now is to fully understand and complete a puzzle. To find the man at the center. Both of them have love to find but they are not free without finding it, the rest is about finding Rahi and giving her justice.

....

Part 9 : The secret of Ravi

Satish and Ravi have been drinking a lot of alcohol in Daman and talking while sitting there. But when it is time for the hotel to close after midnight, the hotel men try to get them out and they both come out. Then those people the bike ride it but there is no balance. Now in such a problem both of them had to reach home. Those people get out but forget the way, then they take another way instead of coming from Vapi. In a drunken state he cannot know the way. It also happens that instead of Vapi, another road is taken, so the road to Umargam is taken. Leaving Daman, he takes the road to Hanuman Dada Kalgam temple of Nargol and reaches Umargam from the back road. When these two ghosts from Umargam arrive at the side of the house, it is half past twelve in the night, the bike stops at the same side of the house.

"Leave it now, bike off." Ravi said.

"Nothing. I'm going to sleep on a bench here. We'll leave in the morning. Let's go to bed here now. " Satish said.

"Brother, you are so tight, I have to find a way." Ravi said.

Then Ravi's eye falls on the ghost house.

"This house doesn't look closed, it would be nice to get something from this house. Let's go to this house, Satish. If we find something, it is good. We will get a place to sleep. " Ravi said.

"Yes, let's go then." Satish said.

Then a man comes to some distance outside the house and he sees these two people going into the house.

"Brothers, don't go into that house, that house is made of curses. All its walls are cursed. Stay away from that house. The ghost spirit lives in that house. You can't come out if you go home. Your body will be found in the morning. " The man said.

"My Sister is not in this world, we are about to die right now. We are going to die. What else?" Satish speaks while he is drunk, ignoring the man's words.

"Should I go in?" Ravi said.

Then the two of them open the answer door inside. The door closes like a few go inside.

"Hey, this is what happened, Ravi Bhai, get out, open this." Satish said while trying to open the door.

"It won't open now, let's go home." Ravi said.

There comes a flying stick from behind Ravi which Satish sees.

"Come down Ravi, the stick has come." Satish said with complete panic.

"This house, That is what must have happened. It seems to me that I must have come here someday." Ravi said.

"How did you come to Gujarat when you first saw it? But my whole being is torn this time. " Satish said.

Then it happens that if these two are standing, then Jummar falls from above, then both fall against each other. So there is a glass attack on Ravini. So Satish is attacked by some bricks. If it beats a little, it screams where it falls. Both of them have something on their head and feet. Both are in great pain. Even so, owning one is still beyond the reach of the average person. Ravi sees some things that get stuck But from there, Ravi suddenly disappears and starts running in panic, So he doesn't know that there is a whole glass plate in front of him which is visible through, So by mistake it hits him and it hurts him a lot. So all of a sudden he sees a girl and tries to go after her. At that moment Satish gets up and sees a ladder in front of her. So the Ravi appears above but it is not the one whose appearance is different, it looks bloody, So he thinks that if something happens to Ravi, he screams and leaves, but arrives like a bad situation. Takes on a monstrous form of ghost, Seeing him, he immediately run in the opposite direction and ghosts started appearing everywhere. So he runs to a room. Where Ravi has already reached and he has written a lot on the wall of the room and on the loose papers. Ravi can't recognize the letter on the wall but the papers in his hand show Satish.

"Let's see, Rahi has written." Ravi said.

"Ravi, why do you know that this letter belongs to Rahi, who are you, who knows Rahi in any way, You has never come to Gujarat, then you has not even seen Rahi and can recognize writing Rahi in any way, why you does not speak." Satish said.

[Who is Ravi telling everything to Satish?]

(Past 2)

Remember the letter? I am the man who took the letter to the canteen. I am the only one who can take off the clothes and the hat. Taking a note that day, I opened my mouth for a moment. And that face was seen by Rita. I felt I immediately hid my face. But when my phone rang over Rahi, Rita told her who the man was and Rahi told Rita everything.

(Past 1 present 1)

"Who are you? Why should Rahi give you that letter?" Satish said.

"Did he see the photo in your house that I said was the necklace?" Ravi said.

"That is my deceiver brother Hemil's. But what do you have to do with it? " Satish said.

Then what Ravi has slapped on his mouth is not slapped, The face looks different so it has a sticker on it. It removes the sticker, removes everything that is attached to the mouth.

"Hemil you!" Satish said in full anger.

"Yes, Hemil." Hemil said.

"You lived in my house and did not let us know. You stayed in our house and dug back." Speaking so angrily, Satish grabs his collar.

After doing so, he starts beating Satish Hemil. Hemil eats a little bit, but there is an older brother, both of them are hitting each other and both of them are talking while hitting each other.

"You came back after separating my house. If this happens to my sister with you, then it is sin for my house." Satish said while beating.

"Satish, I am not a sin, the truth is not what you see from the people. I was slandered, and you believed the words of those who came to slander me. " Hemil said hitting Satish.

" Don't be ashamed to say this with your mouth! You did such a bad job, so fired you. " Satish s said.

"If my work was wrong, why would Rahi be with me? I have been imprisoned for seven years. While in prison, I made all the plans to come to this house and decide what happened after listening to me. " Hemil catches Satish so that he can't let go and leaves him after talking so much.

"After all this, how can I trust you?" Satish said.

"Rahi trusted by me. For me, that is no longer my sister. So someone has to believe. Once you listen to me, think about why Rahi was helping me? " Hemil said.

"Rahi can understand you, so what happened to you?" Satish said. Hemil laughs a little and speaks of the past.

(Past 2)

Nineteen years ago today. We were residents of Gujarat before. Dad got a job in construction in Kolkata. Then gradually got a job, collected money and became a builder myself. Maybe it was about a time when I was very young, old enough to play. When you were born, I named you Satish. And I was nine years older than you. When I was young, my life was spent in fun. Then the house we were in till now is buy from Kolkata. At that time there were some middle class people living in our neighborhood.

When we were little, we used to have a lot of games with our neighbor's son Sahil in the field of our house. So a lot of boys playing and waking up and having fun is about the day when you come and go but go to sleep, so I would invite everyone to play at home, and even mom and dad would be happy. Not even stopping. That day we would wake up in small talk and stay together.

"It's my turn." Hemil said.

"If he's move is gone then my comes, Then if you forgot, it came back And who will come after you because of your mistake? " Sahil said.

"Hey, hey!" Hemil said.

"If only you had spoken." Sahil said.

"Oh no, you are making it by mistake. " Hemil said.

That's why we used to wake up and Dad would come and explain to us and we would start playing together again. If not now the case of life is understandable. As the days went by like this, I was also very strong in teaching. Sahil and I read together at night and get up the next morning to go to school. Then we will grow up. We grew up and Dad would explain to me a lot about what's going on in the world. It was fun living life. It is happening everywhere. Sahil and I were more brothers than friends. When you were twelve years old then I was twenty one years old, my father made me a civil engineer keeping in mind to save his business and Sahil also became a civil engineer. Then Sahil's condition was a little less so I told Dad and took him with me. We sat together and had fun in my well-paid office. Now Rahi was two years younger than Tara. We all lived with a joint family in Kolkata. Now the time has come for us. Sahil and I and our family thought that we should go to Kolkata and live all day together. Took a look. One day Sahil and I were sitting in the office.

"The government officer is coming to check the details and materials of our bridge, you go there. " Hemil said.

"I'm not going anywhere. You go. I won't go in such heat." Sahil said.

"Hey, You have to go. I'm going to pay bill for the tender for the new bridge." Hemil said.

"Hey, I'm kidding, I'm leaving." Sahil said.

Then he goes out and I will pay the tender bill on goverment office. I left the office. There was a call that the bridge had collapsed and Sahil came under it and Dead. At that time I didn't know what to do. Our group was salvaged from all sides. Didn't know where to go or what to do? On one side Sahil died and on the other side my built bridge went. There was no problem with the bridge collapsing. I dropped everything and went there. Sahil was not known. Tears welled up in my eyes. Then goverment went for material testing and then found that the steel bonding used with C grade cement lime did not hold like OPC cement and the steel used used higher carbon steel instead of using thermal TMT bar which did not lift the weight of the bridge and caused the bridge to collapse.

Then Dad alone checked the material written in his report and it happened that he wrote everything differently from the tender we had put, so I felt that someone was deliberately crime us. Then Dad's warrant came out. Dad was arrested. Then I took the material myself and checked the bridge in our lab. When everything was fine, I felt that someone had done everything with the whole plan. Deliberately also changed the material and papers from the office. When they were taken to court for the first time, they checked the material face to face and after doing anything, they gave a week's time after opposite winning. I kept trying to find everything. I didn't get anything then the thing was that when our business was far ahead a Priyank Mistry was a builder because of us he could not get tender and he had big hands on his head. After Daddy was brought in a fortnight later, I did not see any solution, but I stood up while the judge was punishing Daddy.

"Sir, I want to say something." I stood up and said.

"Yes, come here and talk." The judge said.

"Thank you for putting my case in court." Hemil said.

"Yes, what were you saying?" The judge said.

"After changing the papers from the office, I asked the artisan to apply duplicate material. Dad is not to blame. I thought from which godown the material would be cheaper to bring and the remaining money was to be kept for another bridge so that I could make another tender in my name." Hemil said.

"So you take the responsibility of changing the paper and material?" The judge said.

"I take full responsibility. It is my fault that Sahil is dead. I did it for money and it happened to me. In a few days everything will be fine but I did not know that Sahil dead. " Hemil said.

After that I was punished for fourteen years in Kolkata so India time is seven years. Dad even slapped me. Then they decided to come to Gujarat.

(Past 1 present 1)

I finally came to see Rahi that day. I cried a lot because he was coming to Gujarat. I would play it in my lap and make him big. He was confident that I could not do that. All the other opponents in the house were there, but my father never looked back in front of me. For seven years I was in trouble. Rahi informs me in another way where we are. Taking a selfie on Facebook and posting a photo in a way that shows the space behind. Then he gave me a letter and told me heart bit was written in it.

She wrote in the letter, "How are you Hemil bro. I've been waiting for seven years and I thought you'd come out and try to find me first. But a very good effort is to find me on Facebook after your Dirac came here first. I also thought that if put a hint somewhere, you will understand. Jail is a very bad place but I don't want to go there without any bends. But nothing in the whole world can understand you except me. Leave it at that, let's talk now. Satish lives in a house in Kolkata and his servant is gone in a few days. Satish needs a servant. Do it as soon as you can and yes I will wait for you. I love you Big Brother. "

"Just think, no one but me and Rahi knew what I was going to do. Rahi has helped me a lot. So Rahi was my world. You have all the family members attached to you but my family was empty enough till now. I had no one else. Alas, when I heard that this happened to Rahi, I was in more pain than you. My sister One who was with me was also gone. I'm sorry to hear that nature is taking revenge. I was robbed of everything attached to it. Was it necessary to remove sister? The problem is with me the most. My fur was high but who should I tell?

If the way of life changes, sometimes life is shortened,

If not here's a new product just for you!

I thought I was too big, but looking back no one thought,

There is no one like me in this world, so she also separated and went away.

I lived my life with understanding, then someone misunderstood that understanding,

I sacrificed, I did not see what would happen,

In search of who I am, who is laughing at our trouble,

If anyone was found, he would immediately walk away from me.

If I suffer from my own mistake,

Which has no end?

If the end is the same for me,

When I forget everything, when I am one of you.

Farewell to my time,

What I thought was good,

Don't like so much,

With the idea of who is with,

But now i have to live just to give justice. Then I will go far away from you. Just help find the truth. " Hemil said.

"If Rahi thinks this way, then you are right. All I know is that Rahi will be with you. Hemilbro, I will stay with you and help you find out everything. If you are telling the truth, then the truth will come out." Satish said.

"Before that, we have to find out what happened to Rahi. This is enough evidence to give him justice. First we have to look at what happens next, let's talk about what to do first." Hemil said.

"Yes, that's right." Satish said.

"Thank you for listening to me." Hemil said.

"Right now, there is nothing but listening to you without proof. Let's get this over with first. " Satish said.

....

Part 10 : Rahi's mysterious story.

After both Hemil and Satish have finished talking, he looks in front of the wall where the letter is written anyway.

"This wall can be read, at first I think it is rough." Hemil said.

"Didn't you write the address number in the papers?" Satish said.

"That's the decent thing to do, and it should end there." Hemil said.

Then they both sort the cards by number.

"Now what is read writing?" Satish said.

Then Hemil takes refuge while watching and Satish gets frightened.

"What happened, brother? Why do you look like this?" Satish said.

"The man at the center was found." Hemil said.

"Who is it, say brother?" Satish said.

(Past:2)

Hemil understands Rahi's whole thing and tells Satish.

Throughout this story, when Rahi started the game, she used to say that if Ashish looks bad in front of me, then I will do everything badly for him.

When she was about to go for a picnic, Rahi left the house and Harsh put her in the car and brought her out of the house. It is like a forest behind her, there is fear. At that time, except for Ashish Harsh Jill and Sameer, there was another man whose whole brain was there.

(Past 1 present 1)

"Did Bansi stay at the center and do everything?" Satish said.

"Yes Satish." Hemil said.

"How about that?" Satish said.

(Past 2)

When Ashish saw Rahi in the canteen for the first time, he got up and started walking. Bansi must have gestured. She had already told Ashish about the game to be played after that. After that, Ashish started showing exactly what Rahi wanted. Then he did something that made Rahi feel that Ashish had improved. Later, when Rahi told Mahesh everything, he got it from the poisoned Bansi of Belladio in coffee. Taking out the excuse of picnic, Bansi called Rahi out of the house. Harsh then took her and came here to this house. It was twelve o'clock at night when people other than Harsh got together and raped Rahi, then To take her blood and closed the house from all places. Rahi then committed suicide by writing this.

(Past 1 present 1)

"It means Rahi lives in this house as a soul!" Satish said.

"Yes." Hemil said.

"Then why did Rahi attack us? He did something that would kill me. " Satish said.

"Where did you hit that talk?" Hemil said.

"If so, where did it disappear? All of a sudden, the bleeding stopped! " Satish said.

"She gave us a way to get to this room." Hemil said.

"But we are her brothers, was it necessary to kill?" Satish said.

"No, The plan was to bring us here by giving us the way we were going. And I don't know if there is anything else written on the back, but I will definitely find something else. " Hemil said.

"So you haven't got the whole thing yet?" Satish said.

" As I was approaching, I saw a camera lying down and I saw some recording in it. There was a girl who used to come and cry every day and then she said that I will kill anyone who sets foot in this house. I will kill all who are in the shadow of this house in my fire, The ghost is known a bit so I thought of going after it. After I got this room, there is still a message that goes out of my mind. She was talking about killing everyone, but why did we both survive? " Hemil said.

"Maybe you know we're brothers?" Satish said.

"It could be." Hemil said.

Then something is written on the wall. And it seems to them that Rahi writes but also writes.

Rahi said "I know my dear brother Hemil is here. Brother Hemil, you are my last hope. I have given up, now you have to see. Let me just bring these four and Bansi five to this house. Thank you brother.

"It will happen. What was left in our love, sister, I have never thought that you and I have made a mistake, I have not forgiven. I was the eldest of the siblings. I would have done it and I would have stood in front of you. I would never have let Ashish's plan succeed. She didn't tell me this, so I had to suffer the consequences. In the last breath of Mahesh and yours life, I will take revenge as powerful as the wail that came out of my mouth. Your brother Hemil gives this testimony. I promise I will bring them all here before you soon. This night is not for ghosts, but for my sister revenge time night" said Hemil angrily.

"My sister's killers should not be spared." Satish said with tears in his eyes.

"Don't cry Satish, this is not the time to cry. Now is the time to fight war. It's time to attack face to face. Don't give a tear in the eye if you want to give a hard fight. I have raised Rahi in this hand. I taught her to walk, I taught her to live in the world, I fed her with my own hands and raised her. So the thought must have filled me with anger and love for it. This is not the time to cry.

In this fact of time,

Not to be outdone when it comes to war,

You have to fight, if not this way, then another way,

But don't get loose without a fight.

What situation was waiting!

If I had to kill,

The way you hate yourself in life,

So the brothers will get the answer too, "said Hemil angrily.

(The whole thing happened in the same darkness as the house on Road.)

SEASON 2 COMING SOON.

WRITER : HEMILKUMAR P PATEL